Possessed by innocence

AXIS education

Acknowledgements

Cover design: Oliver Heath, Rafters Design

Illustrations apart from page 21 © Paul Gardiner, 2005. The right of Paul Gardiner to be identified as the illustrator of this work has been asserted by him in accordance with the Copyright, Design and Patents Act, 1988.

Brinsford books are a direct result of the findings of a two-year authoring/research project with young offenders at HMYOI Brinsford, near Wolverhampton. Grateful thanks go to all the young people who participated so enthusiastically in the project and to Judy Jackson and Brian Eccleshall of Dudley College of Technology.

First published in Great Britain by Axis Education Ltd

ISBN 1-84618-006-6

Axis Education PO Box 459
Shrewsbury SY4 4WZ

Email: enquiries@axiseducation.co.uk

www.axiseducation.co.uk

Chapter One

The dead were resting.

The nineteen-year-old opening out a board on top of the grave did not disturb them. Anybody watching might have thought it very strange. A teenager, playing board games in a cemetery on his own!

Lenny shivered. It was cooler out here at night. Creepier, too. He wished his parents were not so against the ouija board. His Mum had hit the roof when she found it in his room.

Why couldn't they be more like his Gran? She did tarot readings for all her friends. If they hadn't been so against it he could have been in his nice warm bedroom, letting the glass tumbler slide over the letters of his board in comfort.

Lenny glanced at the headstone. Clarence Cranwell, 1956 to 2001. He had been young – only 45. He wondered how the man had died.

He took out the glass which he had carefully packed in his pocket. There ought to be some good contacts in a graveyard. "Is anybody there?" he asked.

Lenny made himself comfortable. It usually took a fair bit of time before anything happened.

Almost instantly the glass began to move. He jumped, snatched his hand back and broke into a sweat. The glass moved on its own towards the word 'YES'.

Chapter Two

Lenny left the cemetery at supersonic speed. As he ran, he heard the glass shatter behind him. He sped home and shot up to his bedroom. He needed to think in peace. If he stayed downstairs there would be Mum or Dad or both of them, competing for his attention. Besides, he needed a spliff.

The cannabis was good. It calmed him down. He needed to get his ouija board back. It was a really good board. His Gran had bought it for him.

It was still light. He wouldn't have fancied going back in the dark, but nothing can hurt you in daylight. As he walked through the cemetery gate, Lenny shivered. It didn't feel right.

He stood dead still. He heard the eerie bark of a fox and saw the animal creep through the far hedge. It's just the fox, he thought, and shook himself to combat the goosebumps. But as he walked towards Clarence Cranwell's grave his mouth dropped open. His ouija board was set up on the grave again. And the glass was on top of it.

Lenny stood nervously looking at it. He was certain the glass had broken. He'd heard it. Was this another one? Then he laughed to himself. He'd been in such a panic, he must have imagined the sound of the glass shattering. Or perhaps it had been some lads, throwing a bottle at one of the gravestones.

He squatted down on his knees. The cannabis had really relaxed him. He opened his mouth to speak. But as he put his finger on the glass it began to move. The letters spelled out slowly. C.L.A.R.E.N. ...

Lenny snatched his finger back. His legs couldn't move. His heart pounded loudly. His ears were ringing. The glass began to fill ... with a liquid ... How could it? The glass was upside down!

It glugged in like sticky dark treacle. But it wasn't treacle. The stuff was – red. God – it looks like blood... Lenny's head snapped back. All he could see was a green tree full of leaves.

Then suddenly a man was standing in front of him. It was daylight and he was by the river. What was going on?
He could see the man's mouth move, but he couldn't hear the words. The man seemed to be arguing with him. The man's face twisted into an expression of angry hatred. He raised both his hands and Lenny felt them connect with his chest.

He was falling. As he fell, Lenny felt the knife in his hand. It was covered in fish blood and scales. Somehow he knew he had been fishing. Lenny brought the knife up towards the man's face. He saw it nick the man's chin. He felt a splash of water. His chest tightened. He couldn't breathe. The water was deep. This was silly. He was a good swimmer. Then everything turned blue and he was drowning.

Chapter Three

Lenny's eyes opened. He was in his own bed. What was going on? He looked round the room. How had he got home? Had he really been out last night?

He looked at the bag where he kept his blow. It was empty. God, if he'd smoked all of it he had probably dreamed all that nightmare stuff!

Lenny got up from the bed. What a tramp. He'd still got his clothes on. He tore them off, threw them into a pile and strode into the shower. As he ran down the stairs he realised how hungry he was. He stomped into the kitchen.

"Mum, I'm starving. What's for breakfast? I fancy a big bowl of Sugar Puffs, then a bacon butty."

His mum was doing the ironing. His dad's big boots were by the back door. Dad worked digging graves at the churchyard. It was Saturday, his day off.

Mum looked up. "I've got a stack of ironing to do," she said. "We've run out of Sugar Puffs. You'll have to have cornflakes. I haven't got time to cook you bacon. It's eleven o'clock. If you can't get up at a decent time you can't expect me to serve you food."

"Fuck you!" Lenny shouted at the top of his voice. He lifted his fist up as he flew at his mother. He stopped dead, his mouth open. His mother stared at him. Her eyes were wide open with shock. So were his own. He never swore, let alone hit anyone. How could he threaten his Mum? What was going on?

His father stormed into the room, his eyes blazing. "What the hell is going on? I've never heard so much noise in my life." He looked from one to the other. "It's not like you to shout, Lenny. What's the matter?"

Mum burst into tears. "He – he threatened me! He swore at me then he lifted his fist to hit me. Den, he's never done this to me before! I really think he'd have punched me if you hadn't come in when you did." She was sobbing hysterically.

Was he still asleep and dreaming? He could not believe what he had just said and done.

His father grabbed him by the shoulders and shook him hard. "What's going on, Lenny? This isn't like you. You've never been in any trouble, ever. I can't understand it."

Lenny felt his temper beginning to rise again. He shook himself free of his dad's hands. He turned to face up to his father with clenched fists. His real self struggled to take over. I can't fight my dad. The other Lenny, the one that wanted to fight, sneered. Only because he's massive. He'd flatten me.

Whichever one it was, turned and ran out of the house.

Chapter Four

Lenny walked into his Gran's living room.

As usual, she was sitting at the table playing with her tarot cards. She turned and smiled at Lenny, but her smile faded as she saw the scowl on his face.

"What's the matter, Lenny? You're usually so cheerful. Put the kettle on and I'll make a cuppa."

Over the tea and a big piece of homemade cake Lenny told her how he had nearly punched his parents.

"Lenny, what's going on? Has something happened to you? Have you hit your head or something? This just isn't like you at all."

Lenny remembered his strange dream. He told her about it, and about the gravestone.

"Hmm. Clarence Cranwell. I know that name. He lived not far from here. I remember now. He drowned. He was fishing by the river. He fell in."

"It was no accident. It was murder. That's what I think. That's what my dream or vision or whatever it is was telling me."

"How could you possibly know about an accident that happened more than twenty years ago? That man had no enemies." She stopped to think. "No friends really, either. But who would kill him?"

"I tell you, it was murder! It wasn't an accident." Lenny stood up and leaned over his Gran.

He could feel the anger rising up in him again. Also the feeling of awful injustice.

It wasn't fair. Why wouldn't anyone listen to him? The guy had killed Clarence. He'd pushed the man into the river and drowned him.

Someone had to listen. Someone should care.

He screamed at his terrified Gran, "It was murder, you stupid bitch! I tell you, it was murder!"

His fist seemed to take on a life of its own as he punched her in the face.

Chapter Five

He was possessed, he must be. Why else was he attacking all the people he loved the most?

Lenny ran up the path towards the church with one thought in his mind. The vicar. That was the person who would be able to help him.

As he ran he heard the siren of the ambulance he'd called for his Gran. Thank God they had arrived. He had refused to give them his name when he rang. He hadn't been sure they would send one.

If Gran pulls through she might grass on me. I wouldn't blame her. If I don't understand what's going on how could she? But I'll worry about that later.

A figure in a dog collar walked round the corner. He had dark hair and a dark beard with a touch of white in it. He stopped dead when he saw the panic-driven youth running up the path.

"Whatever is the matter, Lenny?" The vicar stepped back a little when he saw the young man's face.

"You must help me!" panted Lenny. "You know my Dad's always done his best for you. Help me. Please. I think I've been possessed."

The vicar laughed and put his hand gently on Lenny's shoulders. Lenny shook the hand away roughly.

"Listen to me. I was playing on the ouija board in the cemetery."

The vicar opened his mouth as if to talk, but Lenny rushed on. "I know, it probably wasn't the right place, but my parents won't let me at home ... the glass filled with blood – it looked like blood.

"Then I woke up, in my own bed. I thought it was a dream. But now I'm horrible. I keep attacking people. It's getting harder and harder to stop it happening. I've hit my Gran. I've ..."

"Slow down, Lenny." His voice was soothing. "Come into the church and talk to me. Tell me everything."

The vicar led Lenny through the doorway and sat him down.

Lenny poured out his story.

"So you see, this guy Clarence must have been murdered. It wasn't an accident. He's trying to get his revenge through me. But I can't control him. I don't know what he wants."

"Clarence Cranwell's death was an accident," said the vicar, but he looked troubled.

"We – he and his friend were arguing. Things got out of control."

"How do you know? It's not as if you were ..."

An image snapped into Lenny's brain. "It was you! You didn't have the beard then, but I recognise you now. That beard had me fooled. It covers the mark where I cut your face with the fishing knife." Lenny felt Clarence's fury wash over him. His head butted the vicar and his fist punched him in the face.

The vicar's nose exploded. He screamed.

Lenny punched him again and again. The man slumped to the ground. Lenny began to kick him, and only stopped when he heard the sickening snap of a rib breaking.

Chapter Six

Lenny stepped back. His whole body was shaking. He could feel the urge to keep punching. He had to stop himself.

He grabbed his hands together as if he was going to pray. If he held his hands together tightly maybe he could stop himself.

He sank down to his knees and cried out, "God help me! I don't want to kill him. Help me to stop it, please."

He bowed his head saying all the prayers he could remember from when he was little and went to church.

Suddenly there was a slithering sound and the vicar groaned.

Lenny's eyes snapped open. He tried to scream but no sound came. The rage had left him. Now he was terrified.

Something was lifting the vicar.

His body was all battered, bloody and bruised. It flopped as if someone was carrying it upwards. Then it stayed still, hanging in the air. It moved slowly until it was draped over the cross.

At that instant there was a massive shattering sound. Every window in the church smashed into tiny pieces.

Immediately there was a dull sound of thunder. Every pew had jumped up into the air then dropped back into place. It was like a chilling Mexican wave.

As the benches lifted into the air, Lenny was thrown forward. He fell to his knees. The pew crashed behind him when it dropped back into place.

Chapter Seven

Lenny sat back. He had tidied Clarence Cranwell's grave. It was a beautiful sunny day.

"I didn't think I'd be able to pull it off, but I managed it." Lenny looked round to make sure nobody could see him talking to a headstone. "I beat the vicar pretty bad, but luckily I only broke a rib and his nose. All the noise of the windows breaking brought people running. They took him to hospital in an ambulance."

He brushed away a couple of fallen leaves and went on. "I visited him a couple of days later when he came round. I told him I didn't think I could stop myself from killing him next time. The only answer was for him to confess to killing you. He didn't know that you had already gone out of me."

Lenny gave a soft laugh and sat back to admire the work he had done. He fingered the deep grooves of Clarence's name cut into the stone.

"He did confess and the police have reopened the case," he told the grave. "But I suppose you know that already. I can't tell what a dead person knows so I thought I'd fill you in.

Oh, and my Gran's okay. She had a dreadful bruise on her cheek but she was okay. She forgave me, especially when I told her what happened at the church. I suppose you were just so angry you didn't care who you made me hit."

He thought for a few minutes, glad that his Gran was well on the way to recovery. But he hadn't quite finished telling Clarence the rest of the story.

"The vicar refused to press charges on me – you – and the police weren't bothered after he'd confessed to murder. They reckon he'll go to prison. I ..."

"Lenny. What are you doing?" His father's sharp voice broke through his last words.

"Get away from that grave. I think you've caused enough trouble messing about with dead people. I don't want to see you in this cemetery again. Do you hear me?"

"Yes, Dad." Lenny stood up and brushed the last crumbs of soil from Clarence's grave from his jeans. Perhaps his Dad had a point.

Or did he? Life had been very interesting over the last few days, hadn't it? Lenny thought about his ouija board.

Were there any less risky places to use it next time?